Enid Blyton's
SECRET STORY GARDEN

ILLUSTRATED BY ROBIN LAWRIE

TEMPLAR

A TEMPLAR BOOK

Produced by The Templar Company plc,
Pippbrook Mill, London Road, Dorking, Surrey RH4 IJE

This edition produced in the UK for Bookmart Ltd.

First published in Canada in 1995 by Smithbooks,
113 Merton Street, Toronto, Canada M45 1AB

These stories were first published in Teacher's Treasury, Sunny Stories, Let's Read,
Enid Blyton's Book of The Year and Two Years in the Infant School 1926 to 1953
These poems were first published in Real Fairies, The Enid Blyton Poetry Book,
Silver and Gold and other collections 1923 to 1968

Edited by Caroline Repchuk
Designed by Mark Kingsley-Monks

Printed and bound in Italy

ISBN 1-898784-43-4

CONTENTS

REAL FAIRIES

Mummy and Daddy, and Nanny and Cook,
Never see fairies, however they look,
And our gardener says that in all of his life
He's never seen fairies and nor has his wife.

Well, I know the fairies are always about,
Because I can see them whenever I'm out,
And often I've longed for a friend who could see
The fairies and pixies and goblins with me.

And now I have really found someone who can,
For yesterday morning there came a wee man,
He ran up to Pussy and tickled her fur,
And directly she saw him she started to purr.

And when I see fairy folk now, anywhere,
I go and fetch Pussy at once from her chair,
And together we sit in the garden and see
The fairies that frolic for Pussy and me.

THE BROWNIE WHO THOUGHT HE WAS CLEVER
AND HOW HE FOUND HE WASN'T

Once there was a little Brownie called Bron who was hunting for lost treasure. He knew a pot of gold was hidden on Rainbow Hill, but he didn't know how to get there. So he went to the Simple Witch, and asked her the way.

"Go down that path," she said. " It leads to hilly country. Cross as many hills as there are legs on a spider, and you will find a river. Row down the river for as many miles as there are legs on a butterfly. After that count as many oak-trees as there are petals on a wild rose. Climb the last one, and you will see a hill where, if you dig, you will find your pot of gold."

Bron thought her directions rather strange, but he wrote them all down. He said goodbye and went away, humming cheerfully, thinking he would soon find the gold.

Now, Bron was a nice little Brownie, but, like a good many people, he thought he knew everything. For one thing, he felt sure he knew how many legs a spider had.

"I can't think why the Simple Witch didn't say cross six hills, instead of 'as many hills as there are legs on a spider!' " he said to himself. "I suppose she thought it sounded clever! Anyway, they aren't very big hills. I'll soon be there."

When he had crossed six hills he stopped and looked for the river. There wasn't a sign of one anywhere! "The witch was wrong!" said Bron angrily, and ran all the way back to tell her so. But she laughed at him.

"It's you who are wrong," she said, and wouldn't say another word.

At that moment, a spider dropped down from the roof and swung just above Bron's nose. And oh dear me! Bron saw it had eight legs, not six! So he ought to have crossed eight hills! He did feel silly!

He had felt so certain that spiders had six legs. He slipped quietly out of the Witch's cottage.

Over the hills he went again, one, two, three, four, five, six, seven, eight. Then he looked around.

And there was the shining river! He ran down to it, and jumped into a boat. "I'm to row as many miles as the legs on a butterfly," he said. "Aha, Simple Witch, you won't catch me this time! A spider has eight legs, so a butterfly has eight too! That's eight miles I must row!"

He set off. It was a long way, and the eight miles seemed more like sixteen. His arms ached and his head was hot with the sun. But at last he had rowed eight miles, and he looked around for the oak trees. But there weren't any!

"Is the witch wrong or am I?" thought Bron. "I'd better catch a butterfly and count its legs!" At that moment a white butterfly perched on Bron's boat, and he leant forward to count its legs.

"Six!" he cried. "Six! And I've rowed eight miles. Oh dear! Why didn't I count a butterfly's legs first? I thought for sure they would have the same amount as a spider. Now I've got to go back two miles, and I'm so tired!" Back he rowed for two miles, and sure enough, there were the oak trees.

"Now I've got to count as many trees as there are petals on a wild rose," said Bron. "I'm going to pick a wild rose and see how many petals it has first!"

He jumped out of his boat and went to a wild rose bush. He picked the first rose he saw, counted its petals, and stuck it into his buttonhole.

"Four!" he cried. "Now I'll count
four trees and climb the last one.
Then I'll see the hill where the gold is
hidden!" So he counted four trees and
climbed the last. But there was no hill
to be seen! Not a sign of one! Bron
was very angry indeed.

"I counted the petals!" he cried. "So the horrid old Witch is wrong! I'll go back
and tell her so!"

He rowed back for six miles, and crossed the eight hills. Then up the path he
went, and burst into the Witch's cottage. She was talking to another brownie, and
was telling him the way to go to find the hidden gold.

"It's no good going!" stormed Bron. "I've been, and it's all wrong! The Witch
doesn't know." The Witch smiled and said nothing.

"Well, I'll see for myself," said the other brownie, catching a spider and counting
its legs. "I'll come back tomorrow and tell you how I got on. Goodbye!"

"I'll come back tomorrow too!" said Bron to the Witch. "And perhaps you'll
admit you are wrong when we both tell you!"

As he went home, his wild rose petals began to fall – one, two, three, four.

Next day Bron went to the Witch's cottage. There was no sign of the other brownie. "Aha!" said Bron. "Your directions were as wrong for him as for me! He can climb the tree and look for as long as he likes, but he won't see a hill anywhere!"

The old witch stirred her pot and said nothing. Presently she lifted her head and listened. Bron listened too. Yes, someone was coming. Who could it be? Perhaps it was the other brownie coming back to say he had been given the wrong directions too. The footsteps came nearer, and then Bron saw that it was the other brownie.

And he had got a pot of gold!

"Where did you get that from?" asked Bron in astonishment.

"From the Rainbow Hill of course," said the brownie. "I crossed eight hills, rowed six miles, climbed the fifth oak-tree, and from there saw the top of the hill away in the distance. The rest was easy."

"Climbed the fifth tree!" said Bron. "But I climbed the fourth! Wild roses have four petals, not five, and the Witch said 'count as many trees as there are petals on a wild rose,' didn't she?"

"Yes," said the brownie, laughing. "But you must have counted the petals of a rose that was nearly over! The petals fall one by one, you know, silly! Dear me, and I thought you were so clever, Bron! Fancy not counting the petals of two or three wild roses, to make sure of the right number!"

Bron remembered how his petals had fallen as he went home, and he blushed red and looked at the Simple Witch.

"I beg your pardon," he said. "You were right, and I was wrong. I'm not as clever as I thought I was!"

"Nobody ever is," said the Simple Witch, and wouldn't say another word.

And what I'd like to know is this: Would you have found the pot of gold or wouldn't you? I wonder!

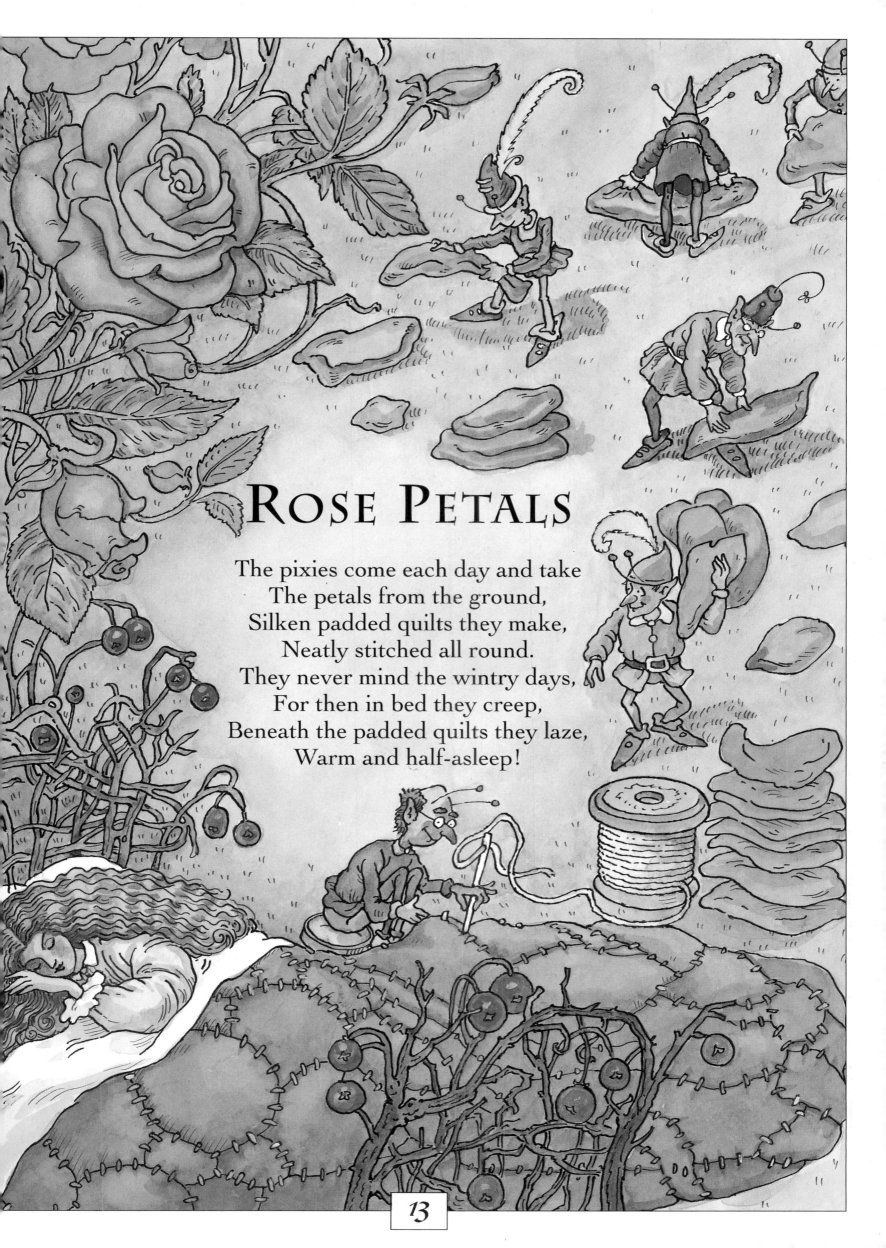

ROSE PETALS

The pixies come each day and take
The petals from the ground,
Silken padded quilts they make,
Neatly stitched all round.
They never mind the wintry days,
For then in bed they creep,
Beneath the padded quilts they laze,
Warm and half-asleep!

THE SPICK-AND-SPAN STONE

Once there was a little gnome called Pinkie, who was always in a muddle. His bed was never made, his dishes were always dirty, his mats were full of dust, and his garden was full of weeds. He could never find anything either. If he wanted the cloth to wipe up, he would spend an hour looking for it under all sorts of things. If he wanted to write a letter, he could never find his pen.

His neighbours were fed up, because when Pinkie really couldn't find something, he borrowed theirs, and lost that too, which was dreadfully annoying.

In the end, nobody took any notice of him. Nobody asked him to parties. Nobody called on him. They weren't going to bother with an untidy little gnome any more.

Pinkie was very miserable, and wondered what he could do.

Then one day he went for a walk and passed old Mother Bumble's cottage. She had been ill in bed, and now she was trying to put her cottage straight. Pinkie saw an odd person going up her front path. He was long and thin, with big flapping feet and a big nose. Mother Bumble seemed very pleased to see him, and he went inside.

"That looks like the Flip-Flap Man," said Pinkie. "I wonder what he's gone to Mother Bumble's for?" He peeped in at the window and saw a curious sight. They were standing in the parlour, and on the table was a big yellow stone.

"That is my Spick-and-Span Stone," explained the Flip-Flap Man. "Now, we'll soon get your cottage nice and tidy for you, Mother Bumble!"

He stroked the stone with his hands and sang in a funny, high voice:

"Oh, Spick-and-Span Stone, we'll leave you alone. And while we're away, work hard, I pray." Then he and Mother Bumble went out. Pinkie watched them go.

Then he stared in surprise! For the Spick-and-Span Stone swelled and hummed like a top. And all the dust on the table and chairs went rushing out of the window past Pinkie's nose – and bits of fluff flew up the chimney – and the brass shovel and candlesticks suddenly shone dazzlingly bright, and the books all straightened themselves, and even the tablecloth pulled itself straight.

Pinkie's mouth fell so wide open, that he nearly swallowed a pile of dust that came whisking out of the window. Then suddenly the Spick-and-Span Stone became smaller and stopped humming. Its work was done. Everything was tidy.

Pinkie thought of his own untidy cottage, and how nobody was friends with him any more. He longed to have the Spick-and-Span Stone.

"But I know the Flip-Flap Man wouldn't lend it to me," he thought. "Nobody lends me anything now. I'll borrow it without asking, and give it back afterwards."

And the bad little gnome slipped in through the window, snatched the stone, and ran home with it without anyone seeing him. He put the Spick-and-Span Stone on his untidy table and stroked it. Then he sang in a little high voice:

"Oh, Spick-and-Span Stone, I'll leave you alone. And while I'm away, work hard, I pray." He slipped out into the garden, and waited until the humming noise made by the stone stopped. Then he went indoors.

"Did ever you see such a lovely room!" he cried. "Thank you, Spick-and-Span!"

He took it into his bedroom, and it did the same there. Then he put it in the garden, and it tidied up, and weeded in a marvellous manner. Pinkie couldn't see how it was done, because things flew about so. He took it in, and put it on his mantelpiece.

"I don't think I'll return you just yet," he said. "I'll borrow you a bit longer."

Now, that was being naughtier still, and Pinkie knew it. In the morning he got up late, and untidily got his breakfast. "I needn't bother to wash up," he grinned. "Spick-and-Span will do it for me. It can make my bed too." He put the stone on the table. "Oh, Spick-and-Span Stone, I'll leave you alone. And while I'm away, work hard, I pray." Then he went out and waited.

It seemed to him that the stone hummed rather strangely – very high and shrill.

"It sounds as if it were angry," thought Pinkie uncomfortably.

When it stopped humming, he went into his kitchen. It was very tidy – very tidy – very, very tidy. Pinkie was astonished. "Where are my plates and cups?" he said. "Where's my kettle? Where are my books? And where are my apples and sweets?"

Then he stared in surprise – for there they all were, stacked in a neat pile on a very high shelf that Pinkie never used.

"Bother!" he said. "That's a silly trick. You've been a bit too tidy, Spick-and-Span! I'll take you back!" But the stone wasn't there. It was gone, and the table was bare!

"That's odd!" said Pinkie. " I suppose it's gone back to the Flip-Flap Man."

He went out to buy a ladder to reach the very high shelf. It cost him a lot of money, and he was very cross. When he got home, he took down all his things and put them in their proper places. The room looked so nice that Pinkie decided to go and ask Pippit, his neighbour, to come for tea. He got two cups and saucers out, and a tin of cocoa, and he put the kettle on to boil. Then he ran to Pippit's house, and Pippit, having noticed Pinkie's tidy garden, decided Pinkie was trying to be good, and said he would come back with him.

Pippit was most surprised to find everything so tidy. But Pinkie was even more surprised at something. His cups and saucers, kettle and cocoa were gone! Quite gone! He couldn't think where to.

"Dear me, Pinkie," said Pippit suddenly. "Why ever do you keep all your things on that very high shelf?"

Pinkie looked up. There was everything, piled up on that shelf! And when he went to get them down he found his ladder was up on the shelf too! Dear, dear!

"I'll have to buy another ladder," said Pinkie, rather frightened, and off he went, leaving Pippit to go back home again, very puzzled. Pinkie bought another ladder and hurried home. He climbed up it, and brought everything down again. And all the time Pinkie could hear a funny little humming noise!

"That's the stone!" he thought, "and it sounds like it's laughing at me! If only I could find it, I'd soon take it back!" But though he hunted everywhere, he couldn't find it. And everything kept vanishing to that very high shelf! If Pinkie left so much as a knife out of place, it would be gone next minute, and he'd have to climb up and get it. He had to make his bed too, because if he didn't the bedclothes would vanish to the shelf. He had never worked so hard, nor been so tidy, in his life before. And all the time he heard the stone laughing.

At last, when Pinkie had to buy a third ladder, because the other two were whisked up to the shelf again, the little gnome grew desperate. "What shall I do?" he groaned. "This Spick-and-Span Stone will ruin me. He looked round his kitchen. Somewhere that stone was laughing. He could hear it, humming merrily.

"If only I could find you!" said Pinkie. "You wouldn't be here a minute longer! But I don't dare to go to the Flip-Flap Man without you. He might turn me into a black beetle or something – and that would be dreadful!"

But the more he thought about it, the more he felt he ought to go and confess the naughty thing he had done. Besides, it was terrible to live with a magic stone; you never knew what it was going to do next. So Pinkie set out for the Flip-Flap Man's cottage. He knocked gently, and almost wished the Flip-Flap Man was not at home.

But the Flip-Flap Man opened the door, and Pinkie nervously told him what he had done. Pinkie cried and said he was very, very sorry indeed.

"And please, Flip-Flap Man," he begged, "will you take your stone back?"

"All right," said the Flip-Flap Man, "I think you have learned your lesson for taking it. But mind, Pinkie, even if I do take it back, it will leave its magic behind, and if you're untidy you may still find things flying up to that very high shelf!"

"I'll never be untidy again," said Pinkie, and he really meant it.

The Flip-Flap Man went home with him. And there was the Spick-and-Span Stone in the middle of Pinkie's kitchen table! The Flip-Flap Man put it in his pocket and said goodbye. Pinkie heard the stone humming loudly, as if it was very happy.

And after that Pinkie was as tidy as could be, and everyone was delighted. There was just one time that Pinkie was untidy – and that was the day he didn't brush his hair and had a hole in his stocking. What do you think happened? Why, he found himself whisked up on the shelf, and there he had to stay till Pippit called and got him down! I don't wonder he tries very hard to be tidy now, do you?

MIDSUMMER NIGHT

On midsummer night,
When the moon shines bright,
And toadstools grow in a ring,
The elfin men
Will sing in the glen
And the Queen will dance with the King.

The rabbit and vole,
The squirrel and mole,
With violin, drums, and flute,
Their music will play
Till the dawn of day,
While the owl joins in with a hoot.

And into our sleep
The sounds will creep,
And we'll wake by the light of the moon,
And we'll know in the glen
The elfin men
Are dancing this night in June!

HAZEL'S UMBRELLA

Hazel had a fine new umbrella. She was very proud of it, for it was a pretty green, and looked lovely when it was put up. She did wish it would rain – but the days were fine and sunny, and it seemed she would never be able to use it. "Go into the garden and pretend it is raining!" said Mother. "You can have a fine game like that." So off went Hazel. She looked up at the sky. "Dear me!" she said. "I think it's going to rain! I must put up my umbrella!" She put up her big umbrella. "It is pouring with rain!" she said. She was only pretending, but she really felt as if the rain were pouring. "What a good thing I have my umbrella, or I'd be wet through!" She walked down the garden to the lilac bush, which she liked to pretend was her house. "I shall go indoors," she said. "But I'll leave my umbrella out to dry. It is so wet." She left it open on the grass, and went under the lilac bush, pretending to take off her hat and coat. Soon she heard a funny little chattering noise, and she ran out from the bush. The noise was coming from her umbrella. How strange! Hazel peeped around it – and saw four little Brownies hiding underneath! They thought it was a tent and had come to live in it!

"Mother, there are Brownies hiding under my umbrella!" cried Hazel. "Come and see!" But before Mother reached the lilac bush, the Brownies had gone! They were scared and ran into the flower-beds.

"I wish I'd seen them!" said Mother. I wish I had too – don't you?

THE LITTLE CLOCKWINDER

Dickory Dock was the clockwinder to the King of Elfland. The King was very fond of clocks and he had a great many. He liked them all to show the same time, and to strike at exactly the right minute. Dickory Dock was supposed to wind them each night – but he often didn't, and then the clocks went wrong.

One day the King gave him a little magic key. "Look, Dickory Dock," he said, "here is an enchanted key that will wind up anything in the world, no matter what it is – but you must just use it for my clocks. Instead of keeping a hundred different keys, you can throw them all away and just use this one for every clock in the palace."

Dickory Dock was delighted – but, even though his work was now much easier, he still didn't always remember to wind up the clocks. One day the King was so cross that he spanked Dickory Dock with one of his best red slippers.

Then Dickory Dock was in a temper! He would punish the King for spanking him! He thought of the naughtiest, silliest idea imaginable.

"I'll use my magic key and wind up everything in the palace!" he cried. He set to work at once and wound up every chair, big and small, every table, every stool and every bookcase. He even wound up the books, vases and cushions – and when the King and Queen came home that night, what a strange sight met their eyes!

"Bless us all!" cried the Queen, as a table came dancing up to her.

"What's happened?" shouted the King, as two chairs ran up and danced around.

"Look at that stool!" cried the Queen. "It's dancing with my best red cushion! Everything's alive!"

"Dickory Dock has been using the magic key I gave him!" stormed the King in a rage.

"Get away, you clumsy great table, you're treading on my toe.

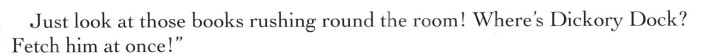

Just look at those books rushing round the room! Where's Dickory Dock?
Fetch him at once!"

Dickory Dock was hiding behind the door.

A footman peeped into the room when he heard the King shouting, caught the
mischievous clockwinder by the shoulder, and brought him before the King. Some
cups came and ran round them, and a saucer rolled all the way up the footman's leg.
It was really most peculiar.

"Go away from Elfland at once!" roared the King in a fury. "Never come back!
Give me your key, and I'll wind you up so you'll have to keep on walking and
never stop. That will be a good punishment for you!"

With that he dug the magic key into the frightened elf and wound him up. Poor
Dickory Dock! He started running and it wasn't long before he reached our land.
He has been here ever since. What do you suppose he does? He winds up the
dandelion clocks, of course! He's just as careless over those as he used to be over
the clocks in the palace, and that is why they are so seldom right! Puff one and see!

THE DANDELION CLOCK

Tick-tock-tick-tock,
Says the dandelion clock,
Ticking out to elfin ears
Days that last a hundred years.
Tick-tock! Time to rise,
Elves and brownies, rub your eyes,
Ugly goblins, bearded gnomes,
Creep from out your little homes!
Tick-tock! Time to play,
Swing astride a bramble spray,
Ride the furry bumblebees,
Tickle toads and make them sneeze!
Tick-tock! Where's your money?
Time to buy a sip of honey
For your dinner and your tea
From a butterfly or bee!
Tick-tock! Time for bed,
Petals underneath your head,
Hush now! Tick-tock,
Says the dandelion clock.

24

BINKLE'S TAIL

Once there was a guinea pig called Binkle. He lived in a cage just outside Jinky the Gnome's front door, and he was very proud of himself.

"My whiskers are fine, my fur is soft, and my ears are pretty!" he said to himself. "No wonder all Jinky's visitors come and talk to me!"

But one day Panikin the Pixie said something that gave Binkle a terrible fright.

"Whatever you do, Jinky, don't let anyone hold Binkle up by his tail. If you do, his eyes will fall out!" he said solemnly.

"Oh! Oh! Oh!" squeaked poor Binkle, hiding himself in a corner. "I do hope nobody would ever do such a cruel thing!"

Jinky the Gnome and Panikin the Pixie laughed loudly, and Binkle couldn't think what they were laughing at. When they had gone, he began thinking very hard.

"Just suppose someone did come and hold me up by my tail!" he thought, "How terrible it would be! I wonder what my tail is like?" He tried to see it, but he was such a plump little guinea pig that he couldn't see anything beyond his humpy back.

"It must be rather a long tail," he said sadly. "Perhaps Panikin was afraid some rude person would swing me upside down by it. Oh dear! What shall I do?"

The more he thought about it, the more he felt afraid. At last he decided to run away that night, go to Snip the Tailor's, and ask him to cut his tail right off.

"Then no one can hold me up by it!" thought Binkle.

So that night, out he scampered, and ran down the road to Snip the Tailor's.

Snip was sitting making a coat for a brownie. "Hello!" he said in surprise. "What do you want, Binkle?"

"Please would you cut my tail off?" begged Binkle. "I'm afraid someone will hold me up by it, and then my eyes would drop out, you know."

Snip stared at him, and smiled. "I'm terribly sorry," he said, "but I'm afraid my scissors couldn't cut off your tail, they're not the right sort. Go and ask Periwinkle the Dressmaker. She's got a fine pair of new scissors!"

"Thank you," said Binkle and scampered off. As he went he heard Snip laughing, and he couldn't think what he was laughing at. He climbed the hill to Periwinkle's.

"I want my tail cut off, in case someone holds me up by it and makes my eyes fall out," explained Binkle. "Snip said you'd got a fine new pair of scissors."

"So I have. But I'm afraid they wouldn't cut your tail off, Binkle," said Periwinkle. "Go and ask at Pippit the Draper's. He's got lots of scissors there."

"Thank you," said Binkle, and ran off as quickly as he could. As he went, he heard Periwinkle laughing, and he couldn't think what she was laughing at.

Pippit the Draper was just shutting up shop, when Binkle came panting up.

"Why, Binkle!" said Pippit. "Why are you out so late?"

"I'm dreadfully worried about my tail," said Binkle. "If I'm held up by it, my eyes will drop out. Periwinkle said you could cut it off, as you have lots of scissors."

"So I have," said Pippit. "But they're all much too small. Why don't you go to the Simple Witch down in the valley? She's got a pair of magic scissors."

Binkle hurried to the Witch's cottage, wondering why Pippit had laughed, and asked for her help. "Pippit said you had some magic scissors. It won't hurt will it?"

"Oh no, Binkle, it won't hurt you at all!" chuckled the Simple Witch.

26

She took a pair of big, shiny scissors. Binkle turned his back to her and waited nervously. Snip! snap! he heard, but he felt nothing at all.

"There you are!" said the Witch. "You haven't any tail to worry about now, Binkle!"

"Oh, thank you very much indeed!" said Binkle, and ran home, full of delight.

As he went, he heard the Witch laughing and laughing, and he couldn't think what she was laughing at. He cuddled himself up in his little cage, and felt very happy.

"Now I'm quite safe," he thought. "My eyes will never drop out. I wonder what Jinky will say. Won't he be pleased to think no one can ever hold me up by my tail!"

Binkle soon fell fast asleep. When he woke next day he tried to look over his plump shoulder to check that his tail wasn't there. But, of course, he was much too fat.

Just then, Jinky came whistling down the garden. But, dear me, he didn't seem to notice anything new about Binkle at all, and he couldn't think why the little guinea pig kept turning his back on him. "What's the matter, Binkle?" he asked at last.

"I've had my tail cut off," said Binkle proudly, "so that no one can hold me up by it and make my eyes fall out! The Simple Witch did it with her magic scissors!"

To his surprise, Jinky began to laugh and laugh, and Binkle couldn't think what he was laughing at. "What's the matter?" he asked, quite offended.

"Oh, Binkle – hee, hee, hee – it's so funny – ha, ha – you never had a tail at all – ho, ho, ho! Guinea pigs don't have tails, you silly!" laughed Jinky.

And then Binkle knew why Snip and Periwinkle, Pippit and the Simple Witch had all laughed so loudly the night before. Poor Binkle!

THE VERY SMALL PIXIE

Pixie, if I were as small as you
I'd dabble my feet in a drop of dew,
I'd make my dresses of spider thread
And wear a daisy upon my head.

I'd swing on the buttercups, golden-high,
I'd ride on a moth or a butterfly,
And if I wanted honey for tea
I'd look in the foxgloves, just like a bee!

At night in a robin's nest I would creep
And cuddle up into his feathers to sleep.
Oh, Pixie, I wish I was small like you,
There'd be such wonderful things to do.

THE PIXIE PAINTER

Pinkity was a pixie painter. He helped to paint the Fairy King's palace one springtime. He had a pot of pink paint, and he took his brush and painted the nursery of the little Princess Thistledown a beautiful pale pink.

He was so pleased with it that he thought he would give the King a great surprise. "I will paint his golden throne pink!" he said. "He will like that!"

So he took his brush and painted the throne a pale pink – but, oh dear me, the King sat down on it whilst the paint was wet, and then what a to-do there was.

"How dare you paint my lovely throne with your nasty pink paint!" cried the King. "Leave Fairyland at once!"

So Pinkity sadly went away and came to our land with his pink paint. And what do you think he does with it? Why he paints the tips of our daisies pink! Have you seen them?

THE FLOPPERTY BIRD

The Flopperty Bird belonged to Winky the Gnome. It was a fine big bird, with lovely long tail-feathers. Winky was very proud of it, and looked after it well.

One day the Flopperty Bird said, "You are good to me, Winky. You may pull one of my tail-feathers out, and make a wish with it!"

Winky was excited. He pulled a feather out, and called his friend Giant Longshanks over to help make a wish. "What will you wish for?" asked the giant.

"Something you can share," said Winky, "because you gave me the Flopperty Bird when it was a chick."

They decided to wish for something they were both very fond of. "I wish for a big raspberry tart!" said Winky.

There was a thud behind them, and an enormous tart, steaming hot and smelling delicious, appeared. They set to work, and soon finished it.

"Thank you for sharing it, Winky," said the giant. Now I must go home, or my wife will be cross."

He was late for dinner, and his wife, who was a witch, was very cross indeed. "Sit down and eat your dinner at once!" she snapped.

"Oh dear. I don't want any," said the giant. "I'm not hungry!"

"What have you been eating?" asked his wife. The giant told her.

"What!" she cried. "You wasted a wish on a raspberry tart!"

"A fine wish it was too!" said the giant. "In fact, I'd like another one!"

"You might have had gold, or a palace, or a kingdom!" stormed the witch.

The giant said nothing more, but the witch thought and thought.

"If the Flopperty Bird has any more wish feathers, it's no good silly Winky or stupid big Longshanks having them," she decided; "I shall have them!"

So that night she took a big pair of scissors, crept into Winky's cottage, and with one snip cut off all the other tail-feathers of the poor Flopperty Bird. He woke up and began to squawk, while the witch rushed away into the darkness.

When she got home she went down to the cellar. She had eight feathers which she flung one by one into the air, each time saying, "I wish for a bag of gold!" Immediately eight large sacks of gold appeared. Crowing and chuckling, the witch went to bed.

Winky and Longshanks were terribly upset about the Flopperty Bird's tail-feathers, but as hard as they searched, they couldn't find out who had taken them. Then one day Longshanks began to wonder why his wife kept disappearing so often.

He followed her quietly the next time she went down to the cellar. And there he stared in amazement at the sacks of gold, for he guessed it was his wife who had taken the Flopperty Bird's feathers. He ran to tell Winky and the Bird.

"Take me to her!" said the Bird. They surprised the witch, who was still in the cellar. "I don't care!" she said, laughing, "I've got my sacks of gold!"

"You haven't!" cried the Flopperty Bird, and he laughed loudly.

"See!" said the witch, and shook a sack open. Out poured a stream of yellow grain! The magic had gone from the gold!

"Aha!" said the Bird. "I think, as you've such nice corn, Mistress Witch, I'll stay a few weeks with you and feed on it, for then my tail will grow again!"

So he did, and each time the witch fed him, the Flopperty Bird gave her a good peck, just to teach her that greediness never did anyone any good!

FIND THE FAIRIES

Jane didn't believe in fairies,
In pixies, brownies or gnomes;
She never wished in a fairy ring,
But stamped on their toadstool homes!

Other children could see them,
But Jane never even tried,
Yet seven live in her garden –
Can you see where they hide?

THIRTY-THREE CANDLES

"I don't want Yah to come to my birthday party," said Twinks. "I don't like him." "Oh, but we must ask him!" said Twink's mother. "He'll be so offended if we don't. He might do all sorts of horrid things to us."

"He's a nasty, horrid, unkind goblin," wailed Twinks. "He'll spoil my party!"

"Well, he'll blow our house down, or make our hens disappear or something like that if we leave him out of the party," said Mrs. Twinks. "Anyway, he'll be sure to do lots of tricks at the party – he's very good at those – just as good as a conjurer."

"I don't like him or his tricks, and I won't like my party," said Twinks, gloomily.

All the same, Mrs. Twinks knew she had to ask Yah. He was a very powerful little goblin, and goodness knows what he would do if he wasn't asked.

The day of the party came. Mrs. Twinks had made all kinds of sandwiches, cakes, biscuits and jellies! She had made a birthday cake, too, with thirty-three candles on it. Although Twinks was very small, brownies are not grown up until they are more than a hundred years old, so thirty-three was really quite young for a brownie.

Yah came with the other guests, dressed in a magnificent sparkling suit.

"I made it of flames, sewn with snippings of moonlight and then damped down a bit with mist," he said. "Nice, isn't it?"

He looked round at the tea-table. "Ah – not a bad spread. Mrs. Twinks. Would you like to see me eat a whole plateful of sausage rolls at one gulp?"

Mrs. Twinks didn't want to see that at all, and neither did anyone else. Those lovely sausage rolls! Everyone wanted one of those! Yah beckoned with his fingers, and opened his mouth wide – and one by one the sausage rolls flew through the air and straight into his mouth! "What a waste!" whispered poor Twinks to his mother.

"Very nice," said Yah, and sat down at the table. He caught sight of the balloons hanging all around the room. "Ah – have you see my new trick of sending sharp looks at balloons – so sharp that they burst? Ha, ha, ha!"

"You couldn't do that!" said Twinks. "Sharp looks wouldn't burst balloons!"

But they did! Every time Yah looked sharply at a balloon it went pop! Soon there were no balloons left. Twinks was almost in tears. His mother frowned at him.She hoped he wasn't going to be rude to Yah. Oh, dear – Yah was such a nuisance!

"Ah – jellies!" said Yah. "Have you ever seen jellies playing leap-frog?"

"No – and I don't want to," said Twinks, crossly. "Leave them alone!"

But, no – Yah did a bit of magic, the jellies jumped over one another, and before long there was one big mix-up of jellies in a dish, all wobbling and shivering in fright.

THE ELF AND THE SNOWMAN

"It's cold!" said the snowman,
Slapping himself.
"I'll build you a fire!"
Said Tippy the elf.
He brought a few sticks
And set them alight,
He kept up the fire
All through the night.
But alas, in the morning
No snowman was there!
"Now where can he be?"
Cried the elf in despair.
But there wasn't an answer,
And nobody knew
Where the snowman had gone.
I wonder – do you?

THE FAIRY POLISHER

In the garden one day I was playing
At bouncing my big rubber ball,
When I suddenly saw a black beetle
Come out of hole in the wall.

His back was all beautifully polished,
And gleamed as he ran on his way,
And then I heard somebody singing
A tune very merry and gay!

The song tinkled out in the garden,
I heard it as plain as could be,
"Oh, beetles who want to be polished,
Come here and be polished by me!"

I peeped to see who it was singing,
And there, on the top of the wall,
Sat a dear little, strange little brownie,
With duster and polish and all!

He rubbed and he scrubbed at a beetle,
And made it all glittering black,
And now, when you see one a-gleaming,
You'll know who has polished its back!

THE MAGIC SCISSORS

Once there was a pixie called Heyho, who lived next door to Wise-One, the witch. He was always peeping at what she was doing, hoping to learn some magic.

One day he peeped in at her kitchen window, and saw her making a silk dress. She took a pair of scissors, put them on the silk, then said, "Scissors, set to work!"

And to Heyho's great surprise and astonishment the scissors started to cut out the dress all by themselves. In a few minutes there was the dress all ready to be sewn up.

"My!" said Heyho. "If only I could borrow those to cut out my new suit, how quickly I could make it. But Wise-One will never lend me anything."

Now that afternoon Wise-One went out. Heyho saw her go, and at once he decided to run in to her kitchen and borrow her scissors to cut out his new suit.

"I'll put them back before she is home again," he thought. "She will never know."

Wasn't it naughty of him? He had no business to borrow without asking.

He slipped in at the kitchen door, took the scissors from the shelf, and ran back to his cottage. He set the red silk for his suit on the table, and then put the scissors on it, just as he had seen the witch do. "Scissors set to work!" he cried.

Then snip-a-snip went the busy scissors and soon a little red suit lay on the table, ready to be sewn up. "Stop, scissors!" said Heyho, very pleased. "I'll take you back."

But the scissors didn't stop! Heyho hadn't said the right words to stop them, so they went on cutting. They began to cut up the tablecloth. Heyho was very angry.

"You wicked scissors, didn't I tell you to stop!" he cried, and he snatched at them crossly. Jab, jab, jab. The scissors stuck their points into his hand, and made him yell with pain. After that Heyho didn't like to touch them. He was so afraid they would cut him again. But oh! What mischief they did.

After they had cut up the tablecloth, they flew to the pretty pink curtains, and snip-snip-snip, they cut those into rags. Wasn't it dreadful? Heyho cried with rage, but it wasn't a bit of good, he couldn't stop them.

And then, my goodness me, they flew down to the carpet and began to slash at that too. Heyho wept louder than ever. It was a new carpet, with a lovely pattern of pink roses, and it was dreadful to see those magic scissors snipping it to pieces.

He fetched a broom and tried to hit the scissors; but they were very artful and always jumped out of the way just in time. Next they started on the lampshade.

"Oh dear, oh dear!" wept Heyho, "whatever can I do? Oh! If only I hadn't borrowed those horrid scissors without asking."

Just at that moment Wise-One, the witch, came home. Heyho rushed out in a hurry and called to her. "Wise-One, quick, come here. Your scissors are cutting my home to pieces! Come and stop them quickly. I borrowed them while you were out."

Wise-One looked cross. She walked into her cottage.

"Then you can keep them," she said, "I've another pair just as good. The very idea, borrowing my things without asking."

Heyho was in despair. The scissors were cutting up his blankets now, and the tears were streaming down his cheeks.

"Please! Please!" he said, running into the witch's cottage. "Do help me. I'll dig your garden and weed it for you, if only you'll stop your scissors from cutting."

"Very well," said Wise-One, who badly wanted her garden dug and weeded. She went into Heyho's kitchen and clapped her hands three times.

"Scissors, go to your case!" she cried. At once the scissors stopped cutting, and flew into the next door cottage.

"Well," said Wise-One looking round, "I should think you'll have enough to do to patch up all these things of yours. It will teach you not to peep and pry, and not to borrow without asking. Don't forget to start digging my garden tomorrow."

"I'll never, ever borrow anything again," wept Heyho. And he never, ever did.

PIXIE COATS

I went nutting and I found
Many nuts upon the ground,
Their coats of ragged green were gone,
Now who do you think had put them on?
It must have been the pixie folk
Who made each one into a cloak,
They cut out holes for arms and head,
Then slipped them on and gaily said,
"Our autumn coats are strong and warm,
They're thick enough for wind and storm;
Upon the hazel nuts they grew,
But now they're coats for me and you!"
And where the hazel nuts are seen
Without their ragged coats of green,
Just look about for pixie folk
Who wear them for an autumn cloak!

WILLY AND THE BROWNIES

Mother called Willy a why-boy. Do you know what a why-boy is? It is a little boy who is always saying "Why? Why? Why?" Willy began when he got up in the morning and he didn't stop till he was asleep at night.

"Why is water wet?" he would say. "Why is the fire hot?" Oh, the questions he asked! "Why does the wind blow? Why does the sun shine? Why do my eyes see? Why does the moon shine at night? Why does my cocoa steam? Why – why – why?"

"Oh, dear!" his mother would sigh. "Do be quiet, Willy. You don't listen to any answers – you just say 'why – why – why,' all day long for nothing!"

"Why shouldn't I?" said Willy. His mother wouldn't answer, but sent him out to play. In the garden he saw a crowd of tiny brownies looking at him. Willy was most surprised. He ran up to them and stared.

"Why are you there?" he said. "Why are you so small? Why are you dressed like that? Why are you in my garden? Why…"

The little men frowned at the small boy, and then, oh, dear, Willy was followed by the brownies who cried without stopping "Why? Why? Why? Why? Why?" You should have heard them! "Little why-boy, why, why, why, why!"

Willy ran away, frightened. He didn't like to have "why, why, why," shouted at him like that. The brownies flew all round, still shouting. "Why, why, why, why!"

Willy ran indoors. "Why are you in so soon?" his mother asked in surprise.

"Oh, Mother, don't say 'why' to me!" said Willy. "I never want to hear that word again. I won't say it again myself either unless I really want to know something!"

His mother never knew why he changed – but we know why, don't we?

SPELLS FOR SALE

Spells for sale! Spells for sale!
Who wants a magical spell?
I've one that has come from the Land of Dreams
And one from a Wishing Well.
I've one that will make you as fair as a rose,
And one that will give you gold,
And plenty to stir in a cauldron black
To conjure up dragons bold.
I've a spell to make you invisible quite,
It's never been known to fail,
Come out, little folk, come out and buy,
I've plenty of spells for sale!